The Tale of Tricky Fox

A NEW ENGLAND TRICKSTER TALE

Retold by Jim Aylesworth

Illustrated by Barbara McClintock

SCHOLASTIC PRESS · NEW YORK

With love to the teachers, who are not so easy to fool!
J. A.

To David, Larson, and Kato, with love
B. M.

AUTHOR'S NOTE

For many years I have loved this traditional trickster tale based on the "trading" motif. An early version from Massachusetts, called "The Travels of a Fox," was first collected by Clifton Johnson, and was originally printed in *The Outlook* in 1897. Johnson was one of the first Americans to gather Anglo-American folklore. This version can be found in its original form in *What They Say in New England and Other American Folklore* (Carl Withers, ed.), Columbia University Press, New York, 1968.

Text copyright © 2001 by Jim Aylesworth
Illustrations copyright © 2001 by Barbara McClintock

Library of Congress Cataloging-in-Publication Data
Aylesworth, Jim.
The Tale of Tricky Fox / retold by Jim Aylesworth; illustrated by Barbara McClintock. -1st ed.
p. cm.
Summary: Tricky Fox uses his sack to trick everyone he meets into giving him ever more valuable items.
ISBN 0-439-09543-8
[1. Foxes–Fiction.] I. McClintock, Barbara, ill. II. Title.
PZ7.A983 O1 2001   [E]-dc21   00-035773

10 9   07 08

Printed in Singapore 46
FIRST EDITION, MARCH 2001

Special thanks to Marilyn Iarusso
for her help in leading us to earlier versions of this tale.

The artwork was rendered in watercolor, black ink, and gouache.
The display type was hand lettered by David Coulson.
The text type was set in 16-point Colwell Roman.
Book design by David Saylor

"Once upon a time," began the kindly teacher, "in woods that aren't so very far away . . ."

. . .Tricky Fox was bragging to Brother Fox. "Stealing chickens is too easy!" said Tricky Fox. "I'm going to get me a fat pig!"

"I'll eat my hat if you do!" said Brother Fox. "There ain't no fox in this whole wide woods that can even carry a fat pig."

"I could!" said Tricky Fox. "If I was to fool a human into putting one into a sack for me, I could! I'll show you!"

And Tricky Fox, he picked up his sack, and he ran off into the woods.

Tricky Fox ran, and he ran, and he kept on running until just before it started getting dark. Then he stopped, and he picked up a little piece of log, and he put it into his sack.

Then he knocked on the door of a nearby cottage.

When a lady opened the door, Tricky Fox hunched over
like he was feeble, and in a rickety voice he said:

"I'm on my way to
Bonny Bunny Bay.
The night grows cold,
And I'm so old.
Please let me stay."

The lady felt sorry for him, and she said, "Okay, I'll let you stay, but no tricks!"

"Oh, no!" said Tricky Fox. "I'm so worn out, I can't think of anything but curling up in front of your fire. I'm just worried about my sack, is all. I don't like for anyone to look in it, and I'm too tired to guard it."

"Don't worry," said the lady. "Leave it with me. I won't look in your sack."

"I know you won't," grinned Tricky Fox, and he handed her his sack and pretended to fall asleep.

But before the lady went to bed, she couldn't resist a quick peek into that sack even though she said she wouldn't.

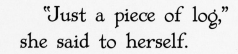

"Just a piece of log," she said to herself.

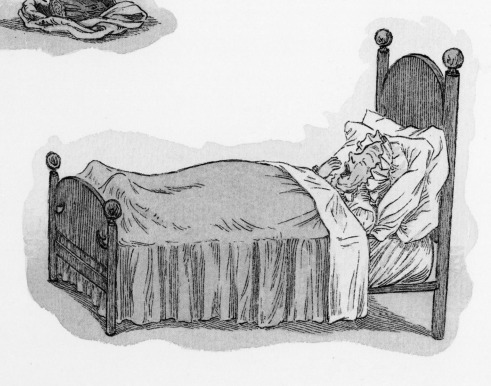

Then she blew out the light, pulled up her covers, and fell asleep.

Pretty soon, Tricky Fox heard her snoring.

Quiet, quiet, quiet, he went over, *tippy toe, tippy toe,*

pulled out that piece of log, and he put it on the fire.

Then, he went to sleep, sure enough.

In the morning, Tricky Fox held up his empty sack, and he said, "What's happened to my loaf of bread?"

"You didn't have a . . ." the lady began to say, and then she stopped herself, remembering that she wasn't supposed to know what was in that sack.

"I don't rightly know," she said, too embarrassed to admit the truth. "Must have been the mice. I'll give you a loaf of mine." And she opened up her bread box and put a loaf of her bread into Tricky Fox's sack.

"Thank you very kindly," said Tricky Fox, and he took the sack, and he ran off into the woods. And as he ran, he sang this sassy song:

"I'm so clever ~ tee-hee-hee!
Trick, trick, tricky! Yes, siree!
Snap your fingers. Slap your knee.
Human folks ain't smart like me."

All day long, Tricky Fox, he hung out in the woods until just before it started getting dark again.

Then he knocked on the door of another nearby cottage.

A lady opened the door, and Tricky Fox hunched over,
and in a rickety voice he said:

*"I'm on my way to
Bonny Bunny Bay.
The night grows cold,
And I'm so old.
Please let me stay."*

This lady felt sorry for him, too, and she said, "Okay, I'll let you stay, but no tricks!"

"Oh, no!" said Tricky Fox. "I'm just worried about my sack, is all. I don't like for anyone to look in it, and I'm too tired to guard it."

"Don't worry," said the lady. "Just leave it with me. I won't look in it."

But even so, this lady couldn't resist a quick peek into that sack, either. "Just a loaf of bread," she said to herself, and she went to sleep.

When Tricky Fox heard her snoring, quiet, quiet, quiet, he went over, *tippy toe, tippy toe,*

took out his loaf of bread. . .

. . . and he gobbled down the whole thing. Then he went to sleep, sure enough.

The next morning, Tricky Fox held up his empty sack, and he said, "What's happened to my chicken?"

"You didn't have a . . ." the lady began, and then she stopped herself, remembering that she wasn't supposed to know what was in that sack.

"I don't rightly know," said the lady, too embarrassed to admit the truth. "It must have flown out the window. I'll give you one of mine." And she took the sack, and she headed out to her henhouse.

When she was gone, Tricky Fox, he danced around, and he laughed, and he sang his sassy song:

"I'm so clever ~ tee~hee~hee!
Trick, trick, tricky! Yes, siree!
Snap your fingers. Slap your knee.
Human folks ain't smart like me."

And when she came back, Tricky Fox took the sack, and he ran off with it.

All day long, Tricky Fox hung out in the woods until just before it started getting dark again. Then he knocked on the door of another nearby cottage.

A lady came to the door, and Tricky Fox hunched over, and in a rickety voice he said:

"I'm on my way to
Bonny Bunny Bay.
The night grows cold,
And I'm so old.
Please let me stay."

This lady felt sorry for him, too, and she said, "Okay, I'll let you stay, but no tricks!"

"Oh, no!" said Tricky Fox. "I'm just worried about my sack, is all. I don't like for anyone to look in it, and I'm too tired to guard it."

"Don't worry," said the lady. "Just leave it with me. I won't look in it."

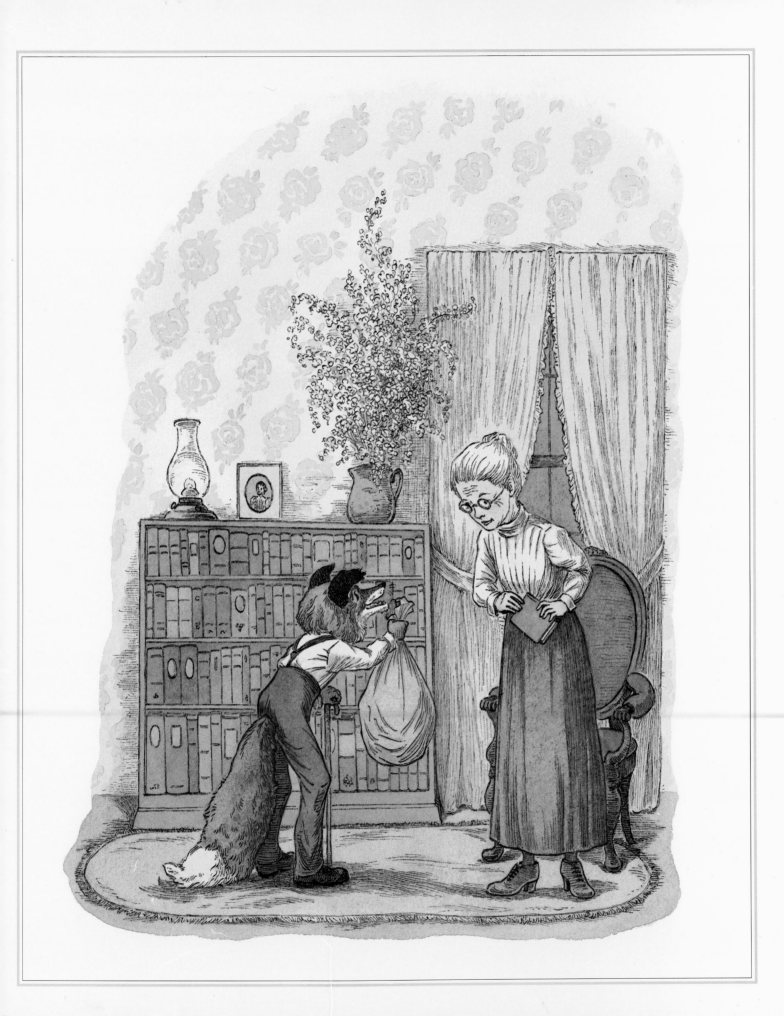

But this lady couldn't resist a little peek, either. "Just a chicken," she said to herself, and she went to sleep.

And just as it had happened before, when Tricky Fox heard her snoring, he went over, quiet, quiet, quiet, *tippy toe, tippy toe,*

and he took out that chicken and he let it loose.

In the morning, Tricky Fox held up his sack, and he said, "What's happened to my pig?"

"You didn't have a . . ." the lady began to say, and then she stopped herself, remembering that she wasn't supposed to know what was in that sack.

"I don't rightly know," she said, too embarrassed to admit the truth. "Must have slipped out the door. I'll give you one of mine." And she took Tricky Fox's sack, and she headed out to her pigpen.

When she was gone, Tricky Fox danced around, and he laughed, and he laughed, and he sang his sassy song:

"I'm so clever ~ tee~hee~hee!
Trick, trick, tricky! Yes, siree!
Snap your fingers. Slap your knee.
Human folks ain't smart like me."

But Tricky Fox hadn't counted on one important thing, and that was that this particular lady was a teacher. And Tricky Fox didn't know that teachers are not so easy to fool as regular humans are. And this lady had gotten suspicious, and she'd come around the side of her house, and she'd watched through the window as Tricky Fox danced and laughed and sang that sassy song of his.

"That rascal!" she said to herself. "I'll fix him!" And instead of going over to her pigpen, she went over to her doghouse.

And instead of putting a pig into Tricky Fox's sack, she put in her bulldog.

And then she brought it back, and Tricky Fox hefted it onto his shoulder and ran off.

When Tricky Fox got home, Brother Fox was waiting for him. And when Brother Fox saw that sack, which looked for all the world like there was a fat pig inside of it, he sadly took off his hat, and, true to his word, he began biting and chewing, and biting and chewing until it was gone.

Then Tricky Fox untied the sack.

And to their sorry surprise, out jumped that lady's bulldog! And that bulldog, he bit 'em low and bit 'em high, and he made the fur just fly, fly, fly! And then, he chased 'em off into the woods.

". . . And because of what happened that day," said the teacher, "every fox in the woods has learned a lesson. And because of what happened, every fox in the woods has been much more respectful of humans. And because of what happened, you never hear foxes singing sassy songs. And because of what happened, you never, ever see one wearing a hat."